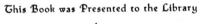

Easy
Gutma

THIS IS A BORZOI BOOK PUBLISHED BY ALFRED A. KNOPF

Copyright © 1999, 2001 by Hachette Livre
All rights reserved under International and Pan-American Copyright Conventions.
Published in the United States of America by Alfred A. Knopf, a division of Random
House, Inc., New York, and simultaneously in Canada by Random House of Canada
Limited, Toronto. Distributed by Random House, Inc., New York. Originally published
in France as Gaspard à l'hopital by Hachette Jeunesse in 1999. KNOPF, BORZOI
BOOKS, and the colophon are registered trademarks of Random House, Inc.
www.randomhouse.com/kids
Library of Congress Cataloging-in-Publication Data
Gutman, Anne.
Gaspard in the hospital/Anne Gutman, Georg Hallensleben.
p. cm.
Summary: Gaspard is taken to the hospital for an operation
after he swallows his new race car key chain.
ISBN 0-375-81116-8 [1. Hospitals—Fiction.] I. Hallensleben, Georg. II. Title.
PZ7.G9846 Gar 2001 [E]—dc21 00-062016
First Borzoi Books edition September 2001
Printed in France   10 9 8 7 6 5 4 3 2 1

Gaspard
in the Hospital

ANNE GUTMAN · GEORG HALLENSLEBEN

Alfred A. Knopf · New York

Last summer, I was Gaspard the Dog Walker.
When our neighbors went on vacation,
I walked their dogs.

And guess what I bought
with the money they gave me?

A key chain with a little race car.

Everyone at school
wanted it, but it
was MINE!

I was scared that someone would steal it. Well, I'm not dumb. I knew the perfect place to hide it. I put the key chain in my mouth . . .

. . . but—gulp—OH, NO!
I swallowed it.
Suddenly, I felt very sick.
Our teacher was worried.
"What happened, Gaspard?"
she asked. But I didn't answer.
I was afraid to tell her
about my key chain.

She called an ambulance.

The ambulance people put me on a stretcher. They asked me what happened, but I still didn't want to tell.

It was a little hard to explain why I put a key chain in my mouth.

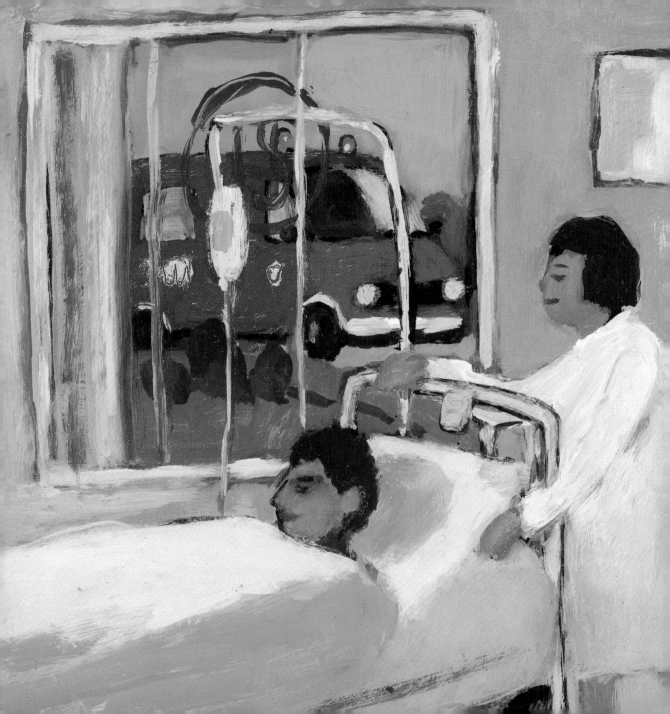

They took me to the hospital.

I had a big room all to myself.
The nurse took off my scarf
and put a white gown on me.
"Don't worry," she said.
"We'll take good care of you.
It won't hurt." But I was
still a little scared, especially
when she took me to
the X-ray room.

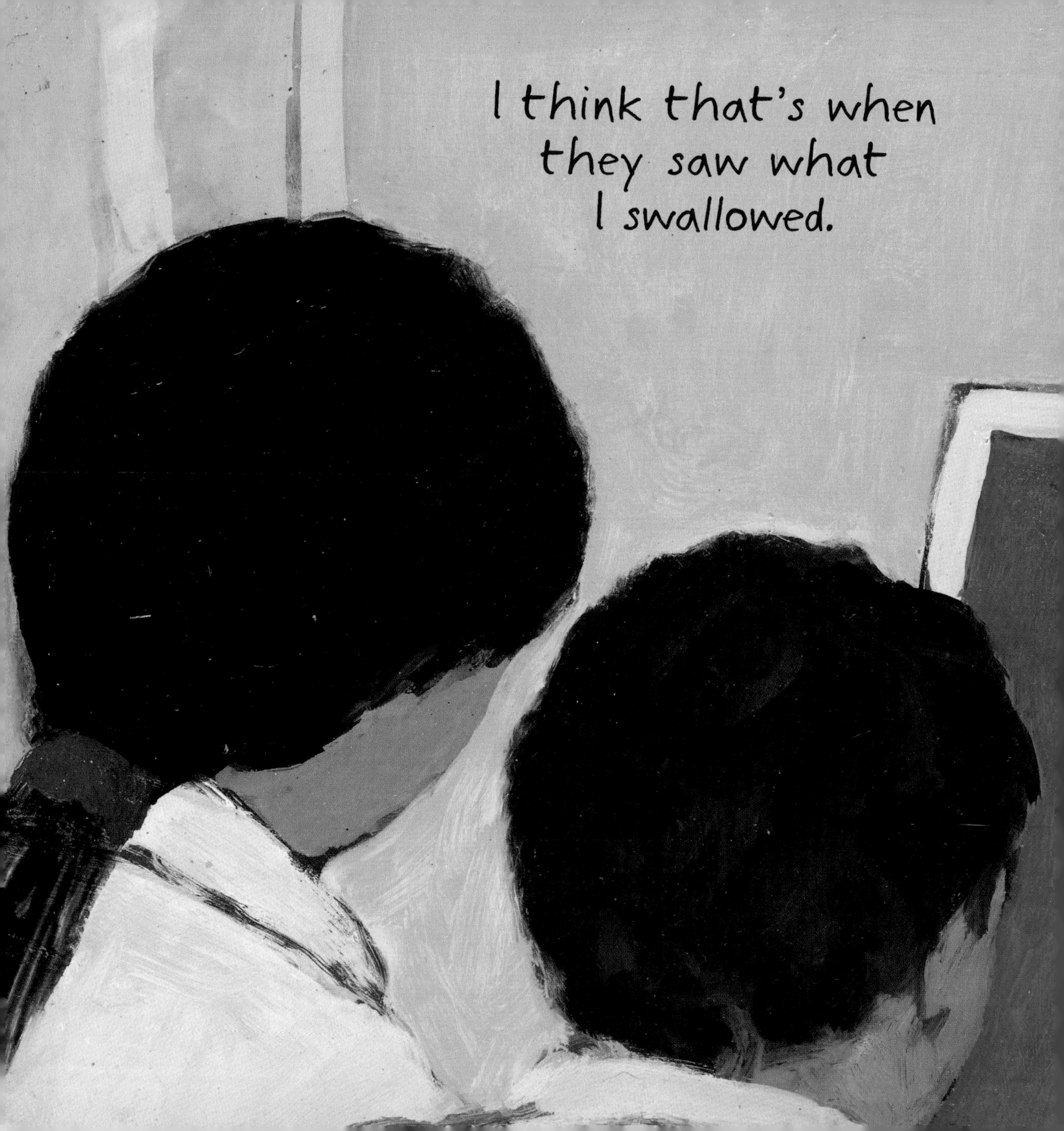

I think that's when
they saw what
I swallowed.

The doctors said they would have
to operate. "You won't feel a thing,"
they said. "You'll be asleep."
"But I'm not sleepy at all,"
I said. They asked me if
I could count to ten.
"Of course!" I said.

"One, two, three . . ."

I fell asleep after counting to three and dreamed I was a race car driver! Vrrroom!

They were right. I didn't feel a thing.
When I woke up, it was already night.

My parents were right there,
and Mom gave me a great big package.

Inside was a race car so BIG,
I would never be able to swallow it.